What's Missing?

In Loving Memory of Jeffrey Leroy
Sleep In Peace!

"If I'm late for this game, I'm going to kill her, Jeffrey, I swear," declared Matthew Loew. From the front passenger seat Detective Jeffrey Jean-Baptiste adjusted his Dallas Cowboys fitted hat on his head then brushed off the lint from his left shoulder while his best friend vented. As Jeffrey was doing the final adjustments to his "game day" attire he glanced at the side of Matthew's face as Matthew stared through the driver-side window at his front door. He stared uneasily, waiting for it to open to his scurrying girlfriend, Ashley. Detective Jean-Baptiste chuckled at the sight of his friend's eyebrows spiking to mirror the Gateway Arch and his egg-white face turning a muddy scarlet. He thought to himself, *Here we go again...take cover...abandon ship...SOS.*

As Matthew Loew tested the loudness of the horn of his black 2013 Acura TL for the fifteenth, sixteenth, and seventeenth time, Miss Taylor, his neighbor, came outside from the adjacent house.

"Stop blowing the horn on your little 'pimp-mobile', Matt," she recommended with a southern slur. "You know that girl heard you the first time you blew your horn and she doesn't give two hoots. You need to leave her alone! You can't take a 'hood rat' out the—" exclaimed Miss Taylor. She was sharply interrupted with Matthew's house door slamming shut and a Clint Eastwood stare from Ashley, the hood rat she was previously chin-wagging.

"That's why he's mine, and your daughter couldn't handle him Miss 'Nosey' Taylor," taunted Ashley. She waved her slender ring finger with the engagement ring on it that Matthew had repossessed from Miss Taylor's daughter and given to her.

Ashley locked the front door then gave her best big-butt ghetto woman walk rendition all the way to the car. Her hips swayed too far away from her body's walking position, she lightly skipped as her hips reached the climax of each sway, and she ever so un-slightly pushed her buttocks up and her stomach out, a simulated walk that came a little too natural to the self-proclaim "classy woman".

Ashley knew her phony stripper walk would anger Miss Taylor since it was, in fact, Ashley who had started the malevolent rumor that Matthew had left her daughter, Ashley, because she was deprived of ample buttocks for Matthew's liking. As Ashley had rumored, "No ass at all."

Ashley wore her jaw dropping 36–24–40 well and let the entire neighborhood know it by not wearing any underwear while she took her morning jogs in a tank top and skintight leggings. "There goes the ghetto superstar," Miss Taylor would say to Ashley as she jogged by every morning. Miss Taylor's scornful stare would follow Ashley from the moment she stepped out of Matthew's house until her shadow disappeared down the street every morning.

"Sweetie! Why do you always take your sweet time when I want to go somewhere that you don't really want to go," asked a now subdued Matthew as Ashley got into the car. "Heck, you even invited yourself this year and you still act like you don't want to go."

"Just drive!" snapped Ashley. "Don't be trying to act all nice cause your quote unquote sophisticated friend, Detective Jeffrey Jean-Baptiste, is around. You probably gonna wanna fight me later about this."

The silent lip biting from Matthew spoke volumes to Detective Jean-Baptiste as he tried to ignore the latest chapter of their verbal squalls. He was becoming accustomed to avoiding their outbursts since arriving in Dallas, Texas, two days ago from Miami. "Can we just enjoy watching my Cowboys beat Matthew's Redskins at Cowboy's stadium without any bickering," reasoned Jeffrey, in his best family judge impersonation. "Matthew, these fifty yard line row five tickets were not easy to come by, especially three together, we may be able to hear the coaches coach if you two call it a truce for a few hours," said Jeffrey.

As Matthew grinned that same childish vindictive yet piercing grin that Detective Jean-Baptiste had known for twenty years since they were nine years old, he knew there was hope for the day after all. Matthew accelerated to seventy-seven miles per hour as he drove unto the onramp of the freeway, and the back and forth banter between the best friends consisted of football statistics and win-loss records for the past twenty years engulfed the trio's trip to the stadium.

Normal sports chatter rang for the next three hours throughout the game without a peep from Ashley who was submerged in her cellular phone sending text messages, gossiping on social media sites, and taking pictures of herself. Life, solely for this routine vacation, as Detective Jean-Baptiste knew it, had returned to normal.

After the game Matthew drove his friend directly to the airport from Cowboy's stadium. Detective Jean-Baptiste liked to be home by Sunday evening so that on Monday morning he could start the business week well rested. At the drop-off zone in the airport he thanked Ashley for her hospitality and punched Matthew in the arm as they got out of the car to bid him farewell.

As Matthew and Ashley sped away, Detective Jean-Baptiste looked through the rear window to catch the continuation of the dispute between the "love birds". On cue it began with Ashley's overdramatic flaying arms and Matthew's index finger finding its target, her nose, after each syllable. Jeffrey laughed as he always did, as he watched them fight. He then proceeded inside the airport with his carry-on in tow.

It was evident that Matthew loved Ashley, but his bravado and promiscuous wayward ways would not let him officially settle down with her like she had been requesting for over a year now. Their engagement was as far as he was willing to go to appease her bickering. The way he would always go back to her after break-ups no matter how many other women would throw themselves at him—perform all the sexual acts she would not, take him on lavish vacations, and spoil him with riches—was the one sign that the dapper Casanova had a heart that beat her name with every pulsation. Matthew's "on and off" relationship with Ashley had been active and eruptive for about a third of those nine years since he moved to Dallas two years after he graduated high school.

The two best friends had enjoyed Detective Jean-Baptiste's yearly trip to Dallas to watch the Cowboys versus Redskins game for nine years.

No matter what case Detective Jean-Baptiste was working on or whatever drunken induced problems Matthew and his girlfriend were going through, they would still find time to enjoy the game.

Since Matthew's move to Dallas he had been working as a journalist for the *Fort Worth Press* as the never-ending first step to catapulting his writing career. What seemed an, impossible task was often discouraging, but Detective Jean-Baptiste would proclaim to his best friend, so he would not give up on his dream, "Your time is coming."

Matthew had an inept and instinctive way of being an a-hole that drove women crazy. At six feet two inches, Matthew would capture a female's attention and soul before she knew his brass side. His perfectly chiseled and bronze, tanned face carried the hint of a Roman god that carried throughout his body. His well-built, broad shoulders carried down the triangle to his thirty-six waist. The years of training at Madison County YMCA's gym had made a lasting impact on his physique, particularly on his sculptured chest, stomach, and legs. Matthew's arrogance was not unwarranted, he knew he was light on the eyes of women, and his opportunistic mechanism almost always took advantage of it.

Detective Jean-Baptiste, however, had a rare intuitiveness and a hindsight that he manipulated into his skill set as the best detective in the Western Hemisphere. Unlike his best friend Matthew, he was not much of a ladies man. He chose to turn down more advances than he accepted; it was the thrill of the chase that excited him. As complex as Matthew was, Jeffrey was equally bland.

Detective Jean-Baptiste downplayed his attractiveness by covering up his physique, often wearing clothing that was one size too big. Always the busybody Detective Jean-Baptiste would not let the constant advances from a woman distract him from his work. He never kept a steady girlfriend, like Matthew, but just an "odalisque" as he often joked with Matthew, a "sex slave."

Detective Jean-Baptiste's face had the very unique and keen roundness of his Haitian ancestors. His gladiator-like physique would show through any oversized shirt he could wear to disguise himself. He could easily be mistaken as being shy with the ladies, but that was a character trait he liked to portray to all his victims before he pounced on them. Slyly a ladies-man, but he most certainly put nothing before his work. He dubbed himself the "Haitian Sherlock."

Matthew always teased that Jeffrey was only able to solve his cases because his uncle in the town of Jeremie, Haiti would do a voodoo ritual on every case and tell Jeffrey who committed the murder. "How else could you have solved all seventy-eight of your cases to date Detective Jean-Baptiste?" Matthew would question sarcastically. Detective Jean-Baptiste would always speak to himself in creole when he got to the scene of a murder for the first time. Matthew thought it was a prayer, but often times, it was an over-used expression of emotion. His favorites were "tonnè" – an expression to describe anger, frustration or disappointment, "mezanmi" – an expression to describe shock and "oh Bondye" – which means oh God.

Detective Jean-Baptiste would not frequent a gym like Matthew, but rather he religiously did one hundred push-ups before every shower. The exercise was effective enough to keep his six-foot four-inch, 225-pound body from going over a pound above his high-school weight. His physique was perfect for the three-piece suits he preferred to wear uniformly every business day.

Rinnnngggg Rinnnnggg…Rinnnngggg Rinnnnggg. After the second ring, Detective Jean-Baptiste answered the phone. He always waited until the second ring. It was an intuitive habit he had yet to give up from using the old caller ID system that displayed the caller's information after the second ring. He was not one for evolving with technology; he had his paranoia. "Matthew Loew (720) 555-6876" illuminated brightly and suspiciously for a 2:00 a.m. phone call on a Thursday morning.

"Someone killed Ashley, Jeff, someone killed Ash..." Matthew whimpered. "I came home from Sally's and she was dead on the floor. Jeff, you have to come find out who did it. Please, Jeff, you know like I know the police here are incompetent. They couldn't rescue a cat out of tree with a ladder or find their own a-holes if their lives depended on it.

"Jeffrey, okay, I'm drunk, I'm hurt, I'm torn, I can't take it, this is like a nightmare in a nightmare. I know we fight a lot but she isn't like the other women I've ever had, she's like the oxygen to my every breath, she's like the next step while I'm walking, she's like my left eye, my left nostril, my left lung, my left ear she completes me, Jeff. I can't stop shaking! She doesn't deserve this, Jeffrey; she deserved a man that wasn't always drunk. A man that would have been home with her instead of out drinking like I was still in that darn community college" sobbed Matthew.

"Mezanmi! I probably love her as much as you, Matthew, cause I know you really love her and she is the only one that has ever kept you calm. I'm hurting here as well. She was just making me breakfast in your kitchen Sunday morning before the game," whimpered Jeffrey.

After fifteen minutes of Matthew's crying and Dallas Police Department bashing, Detective Jean-Baptiste was able to squeeze a few keynotes to help him get a feeling for the investigation.

After they hung up, Jeffrey laid on his bed thinking about the catastrophic news he just received, "*I need some lwil maskriti*" - Lwil maskriti is oil Haitians manufacture from castor bean - he uttered. Jeffrey's mom would always rub some on her hands and forehead to help lower her blood pressure whenever she received news of the death of one of her family members she left back home in Haiti when she migrated to Miami. "*What a sezisman!*" – sezisman is a Haitian-creole word for emotional shock - he uttered while rubbing his head.

 Detective Jean-Baptiste was half dressed and heading downstairs to pick up his pre-packed suitcase that he always keeps in the closet near the front door when he remembered how much he despised working in Dallas.

Detective Jean-Baptiste's hatred was not so much for the city but more so directed toward the Chief of Police, Larry Tunnel, a quintessential a-hole. Detective Jean-Baptiste's first paying case had been in Dallas, and Chief Tunnel had abhorred the fact that the Mayor of Dallas had hired a private detective to solve the murder of his niece. To make the embarrassment of his police not being trusted by their own mayor even worse, the case had been handed over to a no-name private detective with only one solved murder.

"Heck, he is a pup in the business," Chief Tunnel had ranted for weeks after the case was turned over to Detective Jean-Baptiste.

Matthew was assigned to an article on Mayor William Sharp's philanthropist efforts in Southwest Dallas. After the piece got statewide recognition, Mayor Sharp invited Matthew, plus one, to a fundraiser ball for his re-election campaign at the mayor's mansion.

While researching the article about the mayor's philanthropic goodness, Matthew was able to discover some of the mayor's vices and pictures from his perverted weekend getaways to Reno, Nevada. Matthew, insidiously trying to make friends in high places, only shared them with the mayor, after making personal copies in case he needed them at a later time.

The mayor was both electrified and blown away with Matthew's researching skills. The Republicans had spent thousands of dollars extirpating those pictures and anything that placed him in Reno that weekend. Matthew kept any hint of the vacation out of the piece he was writing even though a revelation like that would have gotten him promoted to editor. More importantly, he kept it out of the hands of the Democrats. The mayor instantly immortalized him as a friend and a confidant, having demonstrated the loyalty that went a long way in politics.

The upcoming election was surrounded by the controversy of the unsolved murder of the Mayor's niece, Martha Sharp, his brother's daughter. The democrats, who were never at a loss for words and excuses, blamed their plummet in the polls one month before the election on the republican incumbent getting sympathy votes and the "ignorant voters" not caring about the real issues that faced the city.

By Election Day, the police department had been working on the case for two months without a single clue or stone turned, as the mayor saw it. At the ball, in which Matthew's plus one was Detective Jean-Baptiste, the mayor bumped into the friends while they were exchanging statistics over the prior weekend's trashing of the Redskins at the hands of the Cowboys. As Mayor Sharp shared his take on the game and how he met with coach Blue, the head coach of the Cowboys, the night before the game and gave a few pointers, the bond between the three men solidified and grew with each shared anecdote.

As the mayor shared a particular anecdote of himself on the sidelines of one the Cowboys games with his since deceased niece, he began to uncontrollably cry violently and throw his fists as if the murderer was in front of him. Matthew and Detective Jean-Baptiste swept him through the closest room's French doors so the crowd would not see the mayor in a vulnerable state. After being saved from instant embarrassment and having his manhood and capabilities questioned, he opened up to his new friends about the police department's inability to find a single lead regarding his niece's murder.

Detective Jean-Baptiste, always the opportunist, offered his services to the mayor to timely, in his words, "crack the case" of his niece's murder. After an endorsement from Matthew, the mayor said he would give him control of the case and make the chief of police comply with all his demands in investigating the murder.

In a week's time, as promised, Detective Jean-Baptiste found out that the Democrats had hired someone to rough up the mayor's niece at Nelson Park—where she volunteered in Southwest Dallas. The plan was to make the mayor so disgusted by the attack and with that part of town that he would not hold his yearly book-bag giveaway right before the election. In turn, his sudden cancelation was supposed to sway the democrat voters to not vote for him. The Democrats planned on twisting the story to seem as if the mayor was abandoning his promise to democrat voters in the area.

Southwest Dallas housed roughly forty percent of the democrat voters of a city that historically voted democrat. Additionally, the most influential religious leaders of Dallas were all from the Southwest Dallas area. When running for any office in Dallas all politicians began and ended their campaigns in Southwest Dallas.

Martha Sharp's death, which was not part of the plan, actually had an inverse effect. Not only did he keep his promise to the neighborhood with the book bag drive, his courage under emotional duress and tragedy prompted more people to come out to the book-bag drive. To further add insult to injury, the mayor won the election in the largest margin ever recorded. It was rumored that some of the members from the Democratic Party even voted for the mayor, but, of course, that was just a rumor, a well-flamed rumor by the Republican Party.

Thomas Askew, a diagnosed schizophrenic, had been employed to do the failed kidnapping. His fidelity to the person that hired him rivaled the allegiance of a golden retriever to his owner of twenty years. Even though he confessed, he never told who his actual employer was. Detective Jean-Baptiste could never ferret out even a hint of the intermediary between Thomas and the Democratic Party, leaving their participation void of prosecution.

Matthew was able to place Thomas on the scene the day of the disappearance. His Hunchback of Notre Dame-like physique, oversized dark clothing, cowboy hat, and limp were easily spotted on the County Bank ATM's camera across the street from the park. Hunchback cowboys do not usually frequent the Southwest side of Dallas – an urban area, an easy distinction to raise even slight curiosity.

Thomas lived with his mother, a devoted Republican, on the North side of Dallas – a rural area, where cowboy attire was more prevalent. He had never been to the Southwest side of Dallas at any point or for any reason during his thirty-two years of life, highlighted his mother prior to the confession. The oddity of this person being on the wrong side of town was emphasized and red flagged by Detective Jean-Baptiste as he researched everyone depicted on the ATM camera around the time of the disappearance of the mayor's niece.

The "Haitian Sherlock's" trusted sidekick is Matthew. The two compliment each other as they approach each case from polar opposite rationale. Before the mayor's nieces murder the two have solved one murder and four missing children cases. The murder was not paid but they made substantial money from the missing children cases. Their business and friend relationship was beyond functional, their brother-like bond help with communicating and dictating orders to one another.

Thomas's index fingerprint was found on the Martha's jacket, the jacket was still on her when her body was discovered, out of all the people on the ATM camera from within the one-hour window before Martha's disappearance. Matthew also found out that another mystery print on the jacket belonged to Thomas's childhood neighbor, John Bean. John, however, during an interrogation, claimed he was in the park that day and might have brushed up against the girl.

The Dallas police department did a lot of the groundwork in Martha's murder case; however, they were unable to connect obvious dots.

John, an aspiring politician with a sketchy criminal past, was the connection a private detective could harass without having probable cause. Sadly, though, a viable link could never be proven, John was certainly a pivotal member of the conspiracy to abduct Martha but without Thomas directly implicating him, no jury would ever convict him based on a few un-ended assumptions

If not for the two hours of interrogation and Thomas's mother compelling him to confess, Detective Jean-Baptiste would not have cracked the case. Thomas's confession was a fabrication, but the arrest and consequential conviction was most important. He claimed he tried to converse with the nineteen-year-old girl in pursuit of a date but that she would not entertain the three hundred pounder's advances, so he kidnapped her. He also said that he killed her out of a jealous rage when the girl mentioned she had a boyfriend.

He would not implicate his friend John, but everyone involved with the 2:00 a.m. interrogation knew the truth. In return for his confession, Detective Jean-Baptiste had to promise not to dig deeper into the case, at least not officially, and Thomas was to be sent to a mental facility for the rest of his natural life.

Why she was killed and the Democrats' true intention was never revealed for the record, but Thomas had a long talk with Detective Jean-Baptiste and his mother off the record that revealed a few tips that helped fill in a few gaps. He tried to explain how he did not intend to kill her. She had fought him in the van in an attempt to escape and fell out hitting her head on the concrete. This happened on the way to a safe house where Thomas and John were supposed to hold her until after the election. Thomas would not say exactly, but he was to keep her at the house until after the election was over and let her go. He showed remorse, but ultimately his involvement had caused this young lady to lose her life. His story was confirmed by what the autopsy disclosed so Detective Jean-Baptiste did not question him further; the murderer was apprehended and that was the goal of any private detective.

Detective Jean-Baptiste would always use Matthew to do the fact-finding explorations. He could research and discover anything, absolutely anything. His laptop was his pistol and his laptop case was his holster, and like a real Texas cowboy neither ever left his side. Matthew was a master at his craft. In fact, he was also wise enough to never let anyone know his sources, especially Detective Jean-Baptiste—he called it "job-security." Detective Jean-Baptiste thought that his girlfriend Ashley was his source and that was why, in fact, she always knew how to get Matthew back. It was a bit of trivia Detective Jean-Baptiste did not care to scrutinize.

Detective Jean-Baptiste had a God-given talent of deciphering the most incomprehensible of problems. His ability to be extremely dexterous is why he stayed in amid the action and not behind the laptop like his counterpart. Also, weariness of technology made it an easy choice to keep his friend close in tow. Matthew connecting the fingerprints contributed to the mayor's niece's murder being solved, but it was Detective Jean-Baptiste's idea to check the cameras across the street from the park and cross-reference them with the prints found on the lapel of the jacket that ultimately knocked down the first domino the led to the solving of this case. They solved their second murder case and certain fame and glory were to come of it.

As Detective Jean-Baptiste read over a few notes while waiting to board his flight to Dallas, there was a key piece of evidence that should have been in the preliminary notes that was missing. Detective Jean-Baptiste knew his friend was a creature of habit, and no matter what the situation, there were certain protocols that should be kept. "Those darn Dallas police," he mumbled while taking his window seat in first-class. Detective Jean-Baptiste always sat in first-class, not because he was financially fearless, but rather at six feet and four inches he could not comfortably sit in any other seat on any plane.

Before the plane departed, to the protest of the narrow eyed and sharply sarcastic flight attendant, Detective Jean-Baptiste made a few phone calls, the last one being to Mayor Sharp. "Sorry for waking you

Mayor Sharp, but I need a favor..."

Detective Jean-Baptiste rented a car instead of insisting on his friend picking him up as he usually did on his trips to Dallas. He knew Matthew had his own issues to deal with at the moment. He went directly to police headquarters to see his old grumpy friend Chief Tunnel. The chief had orders from the mayor, so he was expecting some of the chief's not-so-humble Southern hospitality.

After a few hours at the station, Detective Jean-Baptiste proceeded to Matthew's house with two detectives. As he turned on Matthew's street, he called his friend: "I'm here and already on the case, but I think I have something that will blow the case up. Get me the surveillance tapes from last night from the parking lot of the Ripe and Ready supermarket down the street from your house. Get footage from a two-hour window both before and after the time you discovered her body. Once you get them, meet me at Miss Taylor's house in thirty minutes. When you get there, do not knock, just walk in, hand me the DVD and have a seat."

"What are you talking about, Jeff, I'm in no mood to do any work. I...I...I wouldn't know where to start. Everything is cloudy and distorted right now. Is this some voodoo crap your Uncle in Haiti told you? I'm dealing with a lot, can you just deal with it?" explained Matthew.

"Matt, you can have that footage for me in a matter of minutes. You've done it for me a thousand times. Please man! It is possibly the last piece of evidence I may need to actually seal this one. Don't do it for yourself or me but for Ashley's family. Please try to put the sorrow away momentarily, my brother," pleaded Detective Jean-Baptiste.

"I'll try, Jeff," sobbed Matthew. "Wait, so you actually have a clue as to who did it?"

"Maybe. I think the killer is on the tape."

After twenty-five overlong minutes at Miss Taylor's house, she confessed to her involvement in the murder of Ashley. In between sobs and hysterical flops on the ground, she confirmed everything Detective Jean-Baptiste assumed and was attempting to put together while on the restless and fidgety three-hour flight from Miami.

As mystic and "Merlin-like" as it seemed when the "Haitian Sherlock" solved a case, there was a very precise methodical five-question formula he followed to get him started in the right direction. In this case, what got him going was the "what's missing" from the basic information question of his formula. Out of his five questions he always asks each case before starting, the one being void of an answer almost always led him in the right direction.

The difference between a police detective and a private detective is the dedication to one case at a time. A cop's caseload tends to be overwhelming, and the cases often overlap. Detective Jean-Baptiste used a fine toothcomb when filtering and decrypting his cases. It was the basis to his five-question formula that never failed. The questions had yet to fail him since he had instilled them during grade-school missing-pencil investigations.

What was missing from the preliminaries, oddly enough, was Miss Taylor's account of the night. Miss Taylor never slept, at least not a deep slumber. She was the un-deputized neighborhood-watch leader and knew everyone's business on Tree Oak Avenue between Rogerwood Road and Foles Road. If anyone came or went, she would know about it.

The quandary Detective Jean-Baptiste could not decipher during his flight was why would this "headline seeker" clearly leave herself out of the investigation of a murder right next door to her house.

The "I-was-sick-and-sleeping" performance was no match for

Detective Jean-Baptiste's shrewd condescending interrogation. She was like a third grader using the my-dog-ate-it excuse to an Philosophy professor. He read right through her.

Just as she flopped out of the officer's hands, once again during a convulsing theatrical cry, Matthew walked in with an astonished and bewildered look that he radiated toward Detective Jean-Baptiste. He gave an empty hand gesture as if to say he was unable to retrieve the tapes, and then he reluctantly sat down. Realizing what was taking place, Matthew tried to get up and leave. Detective Jean-Baptiste swiftly moved in his way and forcefully sat Matthew down with a powerful thrust from the palms of both hands into Matthew's chest.

Miss Taylor looked at Matthew and began another round of panic-stricken crying. Matthew joined her with his own frenetic sobs. Detective Jean-Baptiste had seen these hollers, yelps, and bellows on many faces before. It usually came after someone was read his or her Miranda rights. However, the writing was all over Matthew and Miss Taylor's face. The two knew they were about to spend a lot of time in jail.

Her confession, through the screams and cries, as sad as it was to hear, shed a lot of hope and much needed explanation. Detective Jean-

Baptiste then replayed the confession to Matthew.

Miss Taylor knew Matthew's schedule better than he did and knew he would be at his Wednesday night "get away" at Sally's bar getting drunk. Sally's was the local watering hole many young professionals in the area went to for their daily release or for help in trying to forget the day's issue(s). As any other bar, it was also a hub for single women looking for a one-night stand. Matthew was the unofficial celebrity among the men in there, because he had the longest active "get the panties" streak, a streak that had been ongoing for three years.

In a vindictive rage that had been mustarding since Detective Jean-Baptiste was in town for the Cowboys versus Redskins game and Ashley was showing off her ring in front of the neighborhood, Miss Taylor had been plotting a way to revenge her self-proclaimed "queen of the neighborhood" title. Because of previous Thursday morning fights with Matthew after he got home from Sally's, Ashley made a pledge with her to never be at Matthew's place when he came home from drinking.

Ashley was one of his catches from Sally's, but he never threw her back in the water. She knew the actual reason why he went there every Wednesday and her protests were never to any profit.

Ashley must have forgotten something at Matthew's house because she was there around 2:00 a.m. Matthew usually came in around 4:00 a.m. so she thought she was safe. Miss Taylor had seen her come in and heard her on the phone on what seemed to be one of her long gossip swapping conversations with one of her "ghetto" friends. In a moment of what she thought was sheer genius, she called Matthew and told him Ashley was at his house with another man.

The bait, as cruel and malicious as it was, was set. Miss Taylor was planning on sitting at her upstairs window for prime viewing to what she expected to be the beating of Ashley's life. That window looked down into Matthew's house and his lightly colored curtains were not much for blocking wandering eyes, Miss Taylor's in particular.

The elder neighbor saw most of the one-night rendezvouses from that very window. Often she watched and envisioned that it was her younger self being taken and loved by her majestic neighbor. Her "Peeping Tom" ways and fantasizing took a hiatus when she saw her daughter in there one Thursday morning.

Miss Taylor never told her daughter because Matthew continued dating her even engaging her, not treating her like his previous one-night stand victims. She also thought it was her, in fact, that used extrasensory perception in bidding for her younger self, her daughter, to be in those sheets with Matthew.

Matthew's five-minute drive home seemed to take thirty minutes. Every time Ashley seemed to be heading toward the front door to leave, Miss Taylor would cringe and drink a long sip of her hot cup of green tea.

She was sitting on a chair stoned-faced next to her bedroom window with her teacup and untouched sleeve of saltine crackers when Detective Jean-Baptiste found her. Detective Jean-Baptiste kicked down the door, both because he knew that the answer to the "what's missing" question in Ashley's murder investigation was beyond the foyer and he and the detectives heard her whimpering like a wounded deer.

When Miss Taylor was found and immediately bombarded with questions, she began to explain how she had "premeditated" the actual murder, at least she assumed so from her vast criminal justice knowledge acquired from watching television detective shows. She explained how Matthew had arrived home about three minutes from the time she called: "The a-hole must have been driving like a man possessed," she explained. As his tires came to a screeching halt, she looked over to the front door to see Matthew on his knees next to Ashley's body on the ground. "The drunken bastard moved so quickly from the car to the house I actually missed the fight. It must have been one quick punch like I later overheard the paramedic assuming when they were trying to revive her," detailed Miss Taylor. "While on his knees I heard him yell into her face, 'oh, my God, baby, I'm sorry, please get up!'"

"Unlike previous times, the tough hood rat would not move. I've seen her take a few good punches and actually fight back. When I seen her lying there motionless after his failed attempts to get her up, I instantly had bolt-tightening feeling in my stomach. At the very moment I knew something was awry, *Jeff*. I was sort of out of it, but last I remember was the paramedic rushing to her side," alleged Miss Taylor.

"When the paramedics pronounced Ashley dead after numerous disappointing attempts to resuscitate her, I collapsed in the chair next to the window," explained Miss Taylor

From the time Miss Taylor collapsed she did not move another muscle besides her lungs and nostrils until Detective Jean-Baptiste discovered her the following afternoon.

"Would you mind filling in the blanks, Matthew?" Detective Jean-Baptiste asked. Matthew's eyes pierced through Miss Taylor's skull like a rattlesnake's glare before it strikes. He then looked at Detective Jean-Baptiste, and in a cracking voice Matthew softly said, "No, let's go downtown."

The police officers, after being directed by Detective Jean-Baptiste, Mirandized the pair then escorted them outside. Detective Jean-Baptiste followed in a daze and was speechless. He assumed his friend had killed Ashley fifteen minutes into their telephone conversation last night, but Miss Taylor's confession still hit like a ton of bricks. Everyone is always a suspect in a murder investigation, especially the significant other.

Detective Jean-Baptiste had maintained his reputation by solving yet another case. However, his best friend was going to prison for much of the foreseeable future. The obvious paradox was why would Matthew call Detective Jean-Baptiste knowing he had killed Ashley.

Detective Jean-Baptiste did not attend any of Matthew's pretrial hearings nor his sentencing; he also did not follow any of the minimal media coverage of the case either. Matthew's mother, being coerced from her son, kept Detective Jean-Baptiste abreast through e-mail, however he never responded to the emails.

Matthew's mother was not upset with Detective Jean-Baptiste because Matthew asked her not to be. She also apprised what their friendship and working relationship stood for. They sought the truth and justice in every case. Matthew had called Detective Jean-Baptiste to solve the case, and she knew her son had had an ulterior motive. Her son's cleverness came from her side of the family.

* * *

Detective Jean-Baptiste had not seen his friend in seven months since the day of Ashley's death when he sat in the back seat of the police car with him on the way to police headquarters. On that day, he did not even go inside the police station while his friend was processed. He sat in the squad car and sobbed for several minutes. After several moments of self-reflection and evaluation, he took a cab back to Matthew's house to retrieve his rental, drove to the airport, and then took the next available flight to Florida.

Now, as Detective Jean-Baptiste went to visit his friend at Dolph Briscoe Unit A Texas State Prison located near the town of Dilley in Frio County, Texas, where he was serving his twenty-year sentence, he planned on getting a response to all the unanswered questions.

Although the case was solved, there were plenty of personal gray areas between the two friends.

Mayor Sharp arranged, through many backdoor favors, to have Matthew housed at a minimum-security facility for the duration of his sentence. Mayor Sharp never forgot a friend and it was evident with this show of loyalty to Matthew. He also knew that Matthew still had the capabilities of burying his political career.

"Fuck you, you fucking prick!" barked Detective Jean-Baptiste as the guards escorted him into the private visitation room. "How could you have put me in such a predicament? I've spent the last seven months as mad as a husky kid on a diet at a Sunday buffet. If I could punch you in the face right now without these guards placing me in a cell right next to you I would," said Detective Jean-Baptiste in a fierce and profound tone.

"Nonetheless, Matthew, I know why you finally requested to see me and I know what you're going to say. You knew you were in trouble, but you also knew that the blame was not solely yours. If you would have admitted to the murder, they would not have investigated it properly and just blamed it on the drunken boyfriend.

"I know you wanted me to get Miss Taylor to admit her participation in the murder. I know you were impressed in how quickly I figured it out, but I won't take all the credit. You left it wide open, you knew the "what's missing" question would have worked in the scenario.

"What shocked me was her twenty-year sentence, but Judge Banks thought she should get the same amount of time as you. I totally agree cause you were pressed into it. I'm not as mad at her as I am at you cause you did kill her, but I think she certainly deserved something.

"I know you were thinking of my private investigation business when you decided to let me solve the case. It was swift and cagy thinking in moments of pure distress, turmoil, and emotional torment. Everything came to me on the flight back home to Florida, but I was still upset, I did not want to see you or hear anything of this case but I am sorry I did not contact you prior to today," explained Detective Jean-Baptiste.

Matthew leaned forward in his chair. "No, Detective Jean-Baptiste, you pretentious a-hole, I did not want to say any of those things. I knew you would have figured it out, you conjurer. I also knew you would still be upset at me even though you puzzled it out. As you have always done whenever I messed up, you clam up then eventually forgive me. Nonetheless, what I wanted to tell you is that I am finally getting the much-needed help for my alcoholism.

"I cannot hide the fact that I am an alcoholic anymore; it's been beyond the point of social drinking for a long time. If I had not been drunk the night of Ashley's death, she would still be with us. My better judgment was impaired, just like the surgeon general warns on every bottle.

"Also, 'Mr. Haitian Sherlock,' the blunt trauma force to Ashley's head that killed her did not come from my hand, as painted by the guileless prosecutor to the judge. Truthfully, she was standing behind the door talking on the phone when I swung the front door open. I crept up to the house to eavesdrop on her with the man Miss Taylor said she was in there with. As I heard her on the phone gossiping with whom I later found out was her cousin Shay, I pushed through the front door. All I heard through the door was 'It was sooo good...' She was referring to the shrimp they had just eaten at their cousin Stephanie's house.

"I never told you, the detectives, my attorney or the judge because I did not want to be charged with any lesser included offense of second degree murder - manslaughter or accidental murder. I deserved the persecution, the scolding from Ashley's parents, and the prison time. The prosecutor painted a picture of me punching her being the fatal blow because my hand was broken, but the injury came from me punching the ground next to her after I checked her pulse and felt nothing. When I did not feel a pulse, it struck my like a pin needle that I just killed her in a jealous drunken rage, I snapped and punched the ground as hard as I could.

"I'm only telling you now so you will stop thinking less of me. I had a problem with drinking, and I'm getting the help I need in here," explained a relieved and resolved Matthew.

The two friends finished the duration of the visitation with details of the pretrial hearings that Detective Jean-Baptiste would not have known of unless he had been there. They discussed possible appealing the sentence Matthew was given. The plea offer he took was an open plea to the judge, he had to admit guilt and let the judge determine his sentence; withdrawing the plea is certainly possible in the State of Texas. It would involve withdrawing his plea and starting the case over, but presenting new evidence that the death was accidental and Matthew still taking responsibility left a strong possibility that he could get a lesser sentence. The friends decided to strategize Matthew's appeal further on future visits since what was most important to Matthew now was getting the help he needed for his alcoholism.

They also exchanged current events and played a timed game of chess. At the conclusion of their visit, they shared an embrace and Detective Jean-Baptiste promised to visit every month.

As the guards escorted Matthew back through the security checkpoints, Detective Jean-Baptiste stared at the "Yellow King" graffiti'd on the seat in which he had just sat. *A seat reserved for a clever mind and constant visitor*, he thought.

Matthew stopped and asked Detective Jean-Baptiste, "Hey, why did you ask me for the surveillance tape from the supermarket down the street from my house?"

Detective Jean-Baptiste smirked and then replied, "I always thought Ashley was your secret research source, and you not being able to produce the tape validated my assumption"

Matthew stared into Detective Jean-Baptiste's eyes while his eyes welled up. He turned around and followed his escort back to his cell with a heavy heart.

www.ingramcontent.com/pod-product-compliance
Lightning Source LLC
Chambersburg PA
CBHW071227130626
46555CB00004B/1880